Avi's Adventures
in the
Mitzvah Car

by
Robin Pamensky
Illustrated by Rita Sadovsky

gefen גפן
publishing house בית הוצאה לאור

Can you guess
What happened one day?
It was on Avi's
Fifth birthday.

Abba and Imma
Bought him a new racing car.
It was yellow and red,
With a big blue star.

Oh how Avi loved
Being a big boy, for sure,
As he drove down the block,
To the park and the store.

On that day he discovered
Something painted on the star
While suddenly he realized,
This was no ordinary car.

It was the number 613,
On the star painted blue.
To remind us of the Mitzvos,
That we all love to do.

Good deeds like Tefillah,
Tzedakah and Mezuzah
So many Mitzvos
We know from the Torah.

And as the day continued
To Avi's great surprise,
This car was not so simple,
It was really very wise.

Avi was being driven
To places that were unknown.
Suddenly he realized
The car was moving on its own!

As it sped away so quickly
Avi kept falling off his seat,
The car raced to do a Mitzvah,
To help a lady cross the street.

On the corner stood a poor man,
Looking sad for quite a while.
So Avi ran to help him
And gave him Tzedakah with a smile.

As this trip continued
Avi found himself once more
Being driven to do a Mitzvah,
At the local grocery store.

A little girl had slipped,
Spilling milk right near the door.
Avi raced to help her clean
The mess up from the floor.

Avi was driven everywhere
To do a Mitzvah near and far.
This was more than something special,
It really was the Mitzvah car!

The car took Avi to the park
Where a little boy was crying.
He couldn't find his bike,
Near the slide where it was lying.

Avi helped the little boy.
They searched far and wide.
Suddenly they found the bike,
Over by the slide.

"Hey, we found my bike!"
Said the little boy with glee.
"I'm so thankful that you helped me
Now I'm as happy as can be."

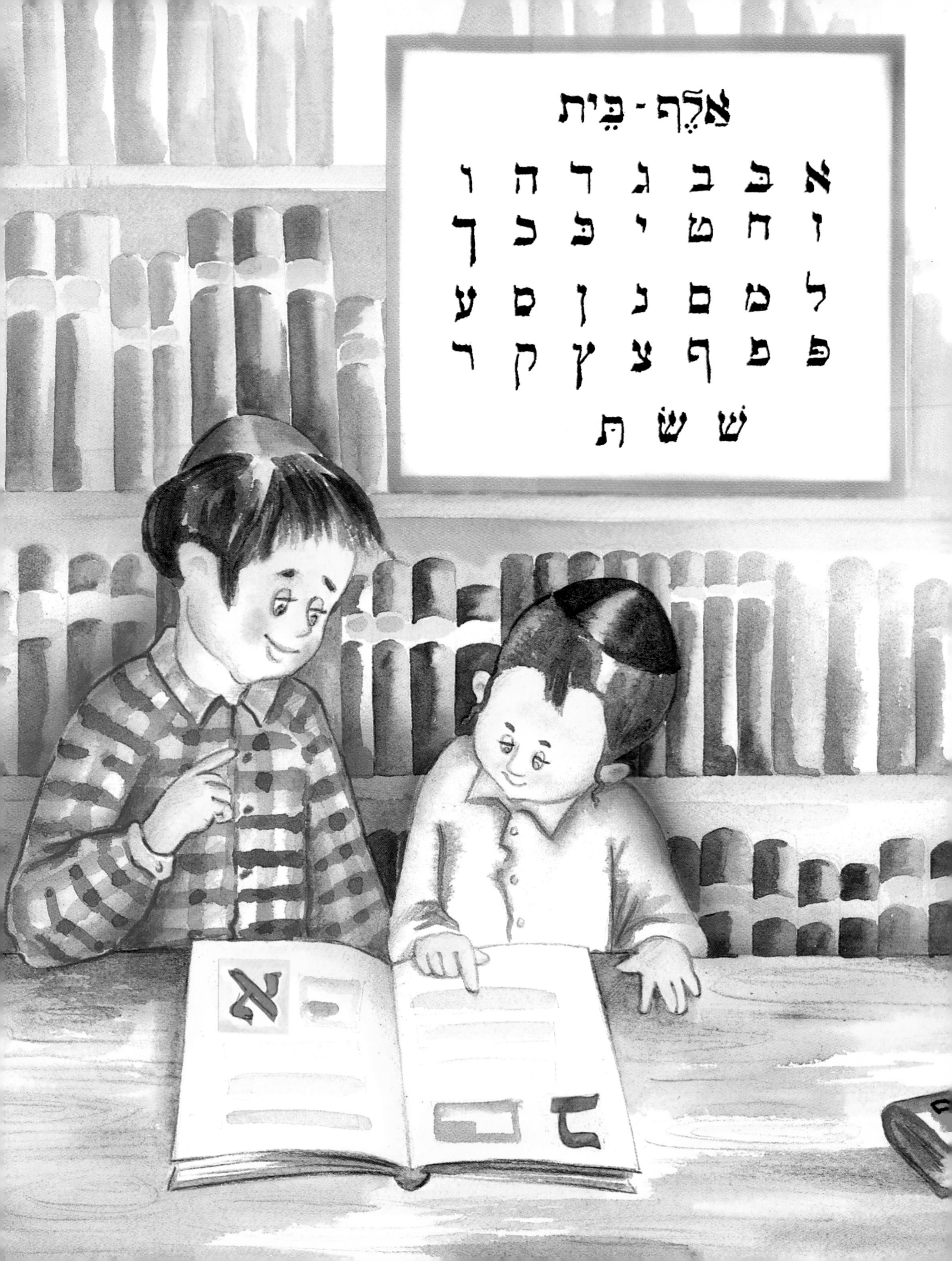
אָלֶף - בֵּית
א בּ ב ג ד ה ו
ז ח ט י כּ כ ך
ל מ ם נ ן ס ע
פּ פ ף צ ץ ק ר
שׁ שׂ תּ

At the nearby school,
Avi helped in so many ways.
He taught a little boy Tefillah
And they learned the Aleph Beis.

Then Avi jumped back to his seat
For he overheard someone say,
"There's a little girl who's sick
In the hospital today."

So Avi decided right then and there
That was a place where he must go.
For he must race to do a Mitzvah
As this car has taught him so.

The little girl was pleased
To have someone come say hi.
She was feeling rather lonely
For her friends were not nearby.

Said Avi, "I'm so lucky,
There's always a Mitzvah to do."
Anytime and anywhere
To help someone, wouldn't you?

All his friends watched
How Avi had such fun.
He loved to share his car,
Happily with everyone.

Avi's fifth birthday
Has been very special indeed!
He's been shown the ways to do Mitzvos,
And help anyone in need.

And now we see, **The Mitzvah Car**
Helps us all to realize,
The many Mitzvos that we too can do
If we just open up our eyes.

Special thanks to
Nancy Lee & Susan Subar

Copyright © Gefen Publishing House
Jerusalem 1996/5756

Typesetting: Marzel A.S. - Jerusalem
Illustrations: Rita Sadovsky

ISBN 965-229-138-2
Edition 9 8 7 6 5 4 3 2

Gefen Publishing House Ltd.
POB 6056, Jerusalem
91060 Israel

Gefen Books
12 New St., Hewlett
N.Y., U.S.A. 11557

Printed in Israel
Send for our free catalogue